Worm sees a flower.

"Smells nice," says Worm.

Worm sees a pine cone.

"Smells nice," says Worm.

Worm sees a strawberry.

"Smells nice," says Worm.

Worm sees a skunk.

"Smells bad!" says Worm.